£3.95

GORDON THE GOPHER™

Annual 1989

CONTENTS

© 1988 Gordon the Gopher Trading Company Limited.
All rights reserved.
Published in Great Britain by World International
Publishing Limited, An Egmont Company, Egmont
House, P.O. Box 111, Great Ducie Street,
Manchester M60 3BL.   ISBN 7235 6833 2

Hello everyone,
Welcome to our first annual. Gordon and I

hello

(that's Gordon). Gordon and I have been friends
for a long...

Hello!

Gordon, do you mind? I'm trying to write the
introduction to our annual.

My anewal!

Pardon?

itz my anewal. Mine all Mine HaHaHaHa Zap!
Powsr at last HaHaHa Pow!

All right Gordon, if you insist. Your annual, but
an annual of your very own is a big responsibility.
I hope you're going to take it seriously.

of coree I will. Are you going to do the introduction
now? Don't forget to give me a big bild up...

Gordon!

Sorry

Ahem. Gordon and I have been friends for a long time
now. We've worked together on TV and we see each other
socially, so I like to think I know him quite well. On
that basis, I can honestly say, with my heart in my
mouth and my fingers crossed, that if ever a gopher
deserved his own annual, it's Gordon. So here it is.
Gordon's annual. I hope you enjoy it.

P.S. I did help him with the tricky bits and made sure
he didn't misbehave.

Brill. Thanks Phillip. I'll do the zame for you
zomeday.

Gordon, what are you doing with that pen? What do you
mean 'last minute alterations'? Put that pen down.
Gordon, come back here...

the AMaZing WOrld of GoRdon

△ I was brought up on the prairie in Central America. This is Aunt Agatha and Uncle Harry when they were young. See that burrow behind them? That's where I used to live.

△ This is Cousin Pablo. He's older than me. He used to tell me tales of the Big Wide World Beyond the Prairie. I decided to go there and seek my fortune.

◁ After a couple of years of travelling I ended up in Britain and found Phillip instead. This is Phillip and me, otherwise known as 'Cute 'n' Furry'. He's my friend. He helped me with the spelling on this bit.

Here's me at Gordonstoun School. I was ▷ sent there for nine weeks by the Gopher Education Concern Organization. It was great apart from the lessons. I joined the Junior Fire Service too. Phillip says I have the right legs for a kilt — short, fat and hairy!

◁ Ha, ha! This is me and my girlfriend, Glenda. She lives in Firmingham with her mum and dad. She's a good laugh. She's dead clever and makes her own clothes and is very fashion conscious. She keeps fit and goes weight training.

△ Aha! This is me, Gopher Party Member for Shepherd's Hedge, after winning the '87 Animal General Election. My 'Popular Policy' defeated the underground movement of the not-really-so-popular Popular Mole Front.

◁ Uh...this is Maurice Mole. A very shifty character and a bad loser. He is the leader of the Popular Mole Front. I don't think he's ever forgiven me for defeating me in the General Election. I wonder if he ever will...

FRAMED

IT WAS MIDNIGHT AND something was burrowing its way towards the BBC Television Centre. It burrowed under the main gates, it burrowed under the car park and it burrowed right under the dozing commissionaire, then it turned left under the canteen and burrowed straight towards the TV studios.

With a quiet scuffling and scraping, the burrower surfaced in the darkened *Breakfast Time* studio, just in front of that rather nice desk that all the guests sit at. Not that you could actually see it, not with the lights being off and everything, but then darkness did not bother the burrower. He was quite at home in the dark, was Maurice Mole. He was the leader of the unpopular Popular Mole Front and arch enemy of politician and TV personality Gordon T. Gopher. And he had not come all this way to collect autographs.

He had a purpose.

Chuckling quietly to himself, he crept up to the producer's box, where all the technical jiggery-pokery went on, and started to meddle about with the banks of controls.

"Ha, ha, hee, ho, ho!" chuckled Maurice under his breath. "This will fix that gopher once and for all. The scandal will ruin his political career. He'll have to resign and they'll hold a new by-election. I shall win and the Popular Mole Front will rise to power!"

Then Maurice Mole gave one final, gloating chuckle, for effect, and vanished back down the burrowed tunnel, leaving the *Breakfast Time* studio all secretly meddled with.

When Gordon T. Gopher woke up the next morning, he turned over and snuggled back into the toasty warmth of the duvet. He was hoping for a bit of a lie in until he saw the alarm clock. It said half past eleven. Gordon sat bolt upright in bed and rubbed his eyes. He had overslept! He should have been at work by nine.

Still half asleep, he came out of the bedroom. The living room in his burrow was a mess. More so than usual. Empty bottles of cactus juice littered the place and the remains of a take-away vegetarian meal sat on the coffee table, looking very sort of left over and not at all appetising. Gordon surveyed the scene through sleepy eyes. It looked like the remains of a successful party, which confused him because he enjoyed throwing a good party and he did not remember throwing this one. Perhaps he would remember when his brain woke up.

"I know I like to keep my past a mystery," he yawned, "but this is ridiculous."

That was when he heard the snoring. It was coming from the bathroom. Gordon stifled another yawn and peered round the bathroom door to see a large, rather chubby gopher lying in the bath. He was snoring away happily .

"Cousin Pablo from Central America!" exclaimed Gordon.

Cousin Pablo had turned up on his doorstep the day before, suitcase in hand, all the way from Central America. He had come to see if his famous cousin, Gordon, could help him. A large building company was threatening to build a huge shopping arcade on the prairie where he and his friends lived. To save their homes they would have to find the money to buy the land themselves.

Gordon, being Gordon, said he would try, then he took Pablo out on the town to cheer him up. They ended up at *Hedgerows,* the poshest nightclub in town. They had their photograph taken for a newspaper and Pablo quite enjoyed himself in the big city. Gordon had eventually got him home after midnight, but only after stopping off for a take-away meal. Even then, Pablo would not go to bed. Instead he got out several bottles of home made cactus juice, which was a lot better than anything Gordon could find in England, and talked about the good old days. It had been half past two before

Gordon climbed, bleary eyed, into bed. By then he already had some idea of how he might help his cousin.

But that was last night. Right now he was late for work. He rushed about the burrow getting dressed, tripping over several plastic bags full of records of Petula Clark singing *Downtown*. They had all been bought in a vain attempt to push Petula back into the charts. It hadn't worked and Gordon had still to find a use for 144 copies of *Downtown*.

As he grabbed a bite of breakfast, he replayed the messages left on his answerphone machine. He skipped over the silly ones left by his friends, listened to a soppy one left by his girlfriend Glenda, and was then quite surprised to hear the gruff tones of the Director General of the entire BBC.

"Never mind all that 'after the tone' malarky, young Gopher," barked the machine. "I want to see you. My office. Twelve sharp. And you had better have a good excuse, or you're fired!"

Needless to say, poor Gordon was a trifle confused. What had he done now? Surely the Director General was not cross about that little prank in the BBC canteen with the cardboard roll, the sticky tape and the *Blue Peter* presenter?

Finally, there was a message from Phillip.

"Beeeep! Gordon? It's Phillip. What have you been up to? Don't worry, it's bound to be a big mistake. There's probably a very good explanation. I'll see you in the D.G.'s office. Bye."

Gordon was quite worried. What was going on? He looked at his watch. A quarter to twelve. Not wanting to leave Cousin Pablo in a strange burrow in a strange city all on his own, Gordon turned on the cold tap in the bath.

"What's going on?" spluttered Pablo, scrambling out of the tub.

"No time to explain," said Gordon abruptly, sticking the sombrero back on Pablo's head and pushing him out of the front door.

"But..." protested Pablo.

"Later," said Gordon, pushing Pablo into the car, then running round the other side and jumping into the driving seat himself. He knew a safe short cut to Shepherd's Bush and the Television Centre

and it was not long before he was flashing his passcard at the security guard on the gate. He parked the car, grabbed Pablo and raced into Television Centre past a mob of reporters who all wanted to ask him questions.

"I know," said Pablo. "You're taking me on a sightseeing tour, aren't you? What's this place, the Tower of London? Will we get to see the Crown Jewels?"

"Later," panted Gordon. He glanced at his watch. It said 11:56.

They made it to the Director General's office with a minute to spare. Phillip was already sitting outside, dressed in his smartest suit, a newspaper folded neatly in his lap.

"Phillip, meet Cousin Pablo. Pablo, meet Phillip," said Gordon, making quick introductions all round. Phillip shook Pablo's paw.

"Ah yes," said Pablo. "You are a Beefeater, no?"

"Well, he's not a vegetarian, if that's what you mean," answered Gordon.

At that moment the door to the Director General's office opened.

"Mr Schofield. Mr Gopher. The Director General will see you now," said the Director General's secretary. Phillip and Gordon filed in solemnly and

Pablo followed them, thinking he was on a guided tour and wishing he had brought his camera.

"Sit down," boomed the Director General from behind his desk. He directed their attention to a television set and video recorder in the corner of the office. "I assume, Mr Gopher, that you are responsible for this?"

He switched on the video. It was a recording of that morning's *Breakfast Time* programme. Apart from a mound of earth in front of the desk that somebody had tried to hide with a spare bit of carpeting, everything looked normal. However, it was not long before Gordon noticed that the little clock in the corner of the screen was running backwards. Then every time a caption appeared to tell the viewer who was being interviewed, or what was coming up next, it said things like, "Gordon T. Gopher is great!" and, "Gophers are best!" and even, "Gordon the Gopher was here!"

Later, when they tried to show the weather map, all that appeared was a picture of Gordon and the words "Gopher Party Rules, OK?"

Gordon was horrified.

Phillip was mortified.

Pablo was bored. He could not find the Crown Jewels anywhere.

"That little prank caused chaos across the nation this morning," boomed the Director General. "People didn't know what time to leave for work, or whether to take an umbrella or not. Utter chaos!"

"But, but, but!" stammered Gordon.

"Don't try to deny it," said the Director General. "You burrowed in there last night and played a practical joke with the caption machine. We found these sunglasses by the hole. They're just your size!" He held the glasses up for them to see.

"They're not mine," said Gordon to Phillip. "Give me credit for some fashion sense, at least. They're absolutely tasteless!"

Gordon was right. They just weren't him.

Phillip thought for a moment. "Gordon didn't do it, Sir," he said. "And I think I can prove it!"

"Huh?" said the Director General.

"Huh?" said Gordon.

Pablo didn't say anything. He was busy looking in the waste paper basket for the Crown Jewels.

"Gordon couldn't have burrowed that tunnel," said Phillip, "because he was out on the town last night." He opened his newspaper at the gossip page, and there was a photo of Gordon and Pablo in *Hedgerows*.

"Well I never!" exclaimed the Director General.

"Also all the spelling in the captions was absolutely correct," continued Phillip, "and as we all know, Gordon's spelling is really rather awful."

"Well if it wasn't Mr Gopher, then who was it, and who do these sunglasses belong to?" asked the Director General. "Who would gain from such a scandal?"

Phillip and Gordon looked at each other.

"Maurice Mole!" they exclaimed.

"Maurice Mole, eh? Dashed nuisance, moles. Wait till I catch up with the bounder," said the Director General. "It looks like I owe you an apology, Mr Gopher. If there is anything I can ever do..."

"Actually, there is something," said Gordon to Phillip. He told Phillip and Phillip told the Director General.

"Capital idea. Leave it to me. We'll announce it to the press chappies downstairs after we've told them that Gordon was the victim of a plot to ruin his career," said the Director General, striding out of his office.

Phillip and Gordon looked around for Pablo. They found him behind a filing cabinet looking for the torture chamber. Gordon grabbed his paw and they all followed the Director General downstairs.

The press were waiting in the foyer and standing near the back was Maurice Mole. He had come to gloat over the downfall of his arch enemy.

"Persons of the press," began the Director General, "new evidence has come to light proving that Gordon T. Gopher was not responsible for the *Breakfast Time* outrage this morning. The culprit was none other than Maurice Mole of the Popular Mole Front!"

"What! But how?" exclaimed a stunned Maurice.

"Look, there he is," said Phillip.

The commissionaire pounced.

"Gotcha!" he said, marching Maurice up to the Director General, who was frantically trying to think up a suitable punishment for him. He had a quiet word with the commissionaire, who smiled and took Maurice down to the BBC canteen where he was set to work washing dishes.

"One final announcement," boomed the Director General to the press. "I am hereby appointing Mr Pablo Gopher sole supplier of cactus juice to the BBC worldwide!"

Pablo could not believe his ears. A business like that could save the whole prairie. "Thank you, Cousin Gordon," he cried.

Gordon smiled modestly.

Cousin Pablo returned to Central America and started a thriving cactus juice business called 'El Cactus Juice Company'. He also made Gordon a major shareholder, which meant that he didn't have to depend on his pocket money from Phillip so much, as he now had a modest private income of his own.

He also had as much free cactus juice as he could drink...

GORDON'S GROANERS

Where do you find a turtle with no legs?
Where you left him.

Why do elephants have ivory tusks?
Iron ones would rust.

What's yellow and flickers?
A lemon with a loose connection.

Why can't a car play football?
Because it's only got one boot.

Phillip: Gordon, how many times have I told
you not to eat with your knife?
Gordon: But Phillip, my fork has got a leak!

What's thick and yellow?
Stupid custard.

What lies in the gutter and moans loudly?
A car with a broken windscreen.
What did the Martian say to the flower bed?
Take me to your weeder.

GORDON? THOSE WERE ABSOLUTELY AWFUL!

Well I liked them. Wait until you see the rest.

YOU MEAN THERE'S GOING TO BE MORE?

GORDON and THE GOPHERTONES

ORDON WAS FEELING BORED.

"Bored, bored, bored," he said, looking round his burrow. He wandered over to his toy box to see if there was anything interesting in there that he hadn't played with recently. It was practically empty. This was because his toys lay scattered around the burrow wherever he had become bored with them. All that was left in the box was a gas mask and an electric guitar.

"Now there's an idea," said Gordon brightly. And so it was — a twelve-inch, chart-topping, remix of an idea. "I'll become a pop star!"

He raced round to tell Phillip.

"I'm going to become a pop star," he announced.

"Don't forget that Glenda's coming up to visit you for a few weeks," said Phillip.

"Oh no," replied Gordon, "I won't. So how do I go about it, then?"

"Go about what?"

"Becoming a pop star!" said Gordon.

"Oh, that. I thought you were joking."

"No."

"Well, first of all you need a good song. You have got a good song, I take it?"

"Er — no, not exactly," said Gordon.

"And you need a band," continued Phillip, "so you'll have to hold auditions."

"Auditions," muttered Gordon.

"Then you'll have to arrange some gigs, do some concerts, that sort of thing. Are you sure you know what you're letting yourself in for?" But Phillip was talking to himself. Gordon had wandered off. Phillip shook his head. "Oh well, I suppose it'll keep him out of mischief for a while..." Then he sighed. "I should be so lucky!"

Back in his burrow, Gordon found a pad and pencil and sat down to write a song. He was only at it for thirty seconds before he got stuck.

"You obviously have to be in the mood," he said, sucking the end of his pencil thoughtfully. He went into the bedroom and slipped into his black biker's jacket, put on his wraparound shades and checked out his moves in the mirror until he felt well hip. Well, hip enough to write a song, anyway.

He'd managed to write three verses and a sort of chorus when there was a knock at the door. He strolled over and opened it. It was his girlfriend, Glenda.

"Hey, Glenda, burrow on down, babe," he droned, oozing cool like a defrosting refrigerator.

"I beg your pardon?" said Glenda, who thought she'd come in halfway through the conversation.

"Er — I mean hello, come in," said Gordon hastily, taking off his shades. Glenda came in and put down her bags.

Over a couple of glasses of cactus juice, Gordon told Glenda about his latest idea. She was delighted to hear that he was planning a career in the music business.

"We could do a duet together," she said.

"Well, actually I was planning on forming a band."

"And what about me? What am I supposed to do?" asked Glenda, who hadn't come all the way from Firmingham just to sit around while Gordon waltzed off to a bunch of silly band practices with the boys.

"Well...uh...you can do the doo wops!" said Gordon quickly.

"Do what?"

"Not do whats — doo wops. You know, thingies. Whatchamacallits. Backing vocals."

It wasn't quite how Glenda had imagined spending her visit, but it did sound like fun, so she agreed.

"Great!" said Gordon.

Later, they went round to Phillip's. Glenda was supposed to be staying in Gordon's spare room, but it was so full of junk that Phillip had agreed to put her up.

On the way back, Gordon placed an advert in the newsagent's window for twenty pence:

LEED SINGER (GOING PLAYSIS)
RQUIRES BAND (TO GO WITH HIM).
ANIMALS UNDER TWENTY INCHS PRFERD.
ORDISHONS TONITE — 6.30 IN MY BURROW.
Gordon T. Gopher.

Unfortunately, he didn't say which night 'tonite' was. Applicants called every night for a week until his twenty pence ran out and the newsagent took his advert down. He suffered tone-deaf singers, drummers who seemed to think they were missing their vocation and should really be doing something dangerous in demolition, and guitarists who sounded as if they worked part time at Heathrow Airport, scaring the birds off the runways.

Slowly, however, an all-gopher band began to form. There was Gaz on saxophone, Mick on bass guitar and Spider on drums. Gordon was lead singer and lead guitar and Glenda was backing vocals.

"So what are we called then?" sniffed Spider at their first band practice in Gordon's burrow. He hoped it would be something outrageously heavy metal.

"Something weird," suggested Mick, "something like 'The Extruded Plastic Yoghurt Cartons', yeah?"

Glenda pulled a face.

"I like 'The Burrowers'," said Gaz.

That was when the arguments started.

"Hold it!" yelled Gordon above the babble of bickering band members. "We're going to be called 'Gordon and the Gophertones'."

There was a moment of stunned silence and before the arguments could start again, Gordon handed out copies of his finished song, entitled *Burrow On Down*. Everybody thought it had something, but nobody was quite sure what. Mick thought it should be really weird with lots of synthesisers, but Spider reckoned it ought to be a heavy rock anthem, with a massive drum solo. Gaz said he'd toot along to anything so long as it wasn't weird or heavy, and they started to argue all over again. Gordon was beginning to wish he'd gone solo or done that duet with Glenda.

When band practice was finally over, the Gophertones packed up to go home. Spider suggested going for something to eat, but they couldn't decide what and they couldn't decide

TWANNG

When they got to Phillip's he was waiting for them. He'd had several complaints about the noise coming from Gordon's burrow.

"Ah, Gordon, I want a word with you, young fella me lad," he said sternly.

"Oh-oh!" muttered Gordon. He knew that look. It was Phillip's you've-been-getting-into-mischief-again-haven't-you? look.

"I've had people complaining that your band practice was too loud. It's half past seven and way past your bedtime, too."

"Oooops! Sorry," said Gordon apologetically. "It won't happen again."

"Just make sure it doesn't."

"It won't," said Glenda, feeling she was partly to blame. "Gordon's band has split up."

"What, already? I gave it at least a week!" said Phillip.

"Well normally I wouldn't mind," said Gordon, "but I've got this gig at *Stringburrow's* next week and I was wondering..." His voice trailed off.

"And you were wondering if I'd help out?" suggested Phillip.

"Well, that depends," replied Gordon.

"Depends? Depends on what?"

"On whether you can make a noise like a drum machine."

"Well, not really. Not so you'd notice," said Phillip slowly. 'But I can do a pretty mean human balalaika. Or how about a Tyrolean horn? I'm very good with those."

"Er...no, I don't think so," said Gordon.

"Look, I'll see what I can do," said Phillip. "Come round tomorrow and we'll sort something out, all right?"

Gordon nodded, sighed, said goodnight to Glenda and went off home.

The next morning he was round at Phillip's bright and early. Phillip and Glenda were just having breakfast when he arrived.

"Morning, Gordon. Fancy some breakfast?" asked Phillip, pouring out a bowl of muesli. Gordon shook his head. He didn't have much of an appetite.

"Cheer up," said Glenda. "We've persuaded the Gophertones to re-form for the concert next week."

"What! But how..." gasped Gordon.

"We phoned them up. All we had to do was say *Stringburrow's* and they agreed like a shot — well, almost."

"Yippee!" yelled Gordon. Then, his appetite returning, he said, "About breakfast. I don't suppose you have any of those sugar-frosted alfalfa flakes, do you?"

where. Another argument broke out and the Gophertones promptly split up, claiming 'irreconcilable differences' and vowing never to work with each other again. Gordon and Glenda watched, stunned, as the now ex-Gophertones went their separate ways.

"But I've gone and arranged a gig at *Stringburrow's* nightclub next week," squeaked Gordon.

He was very quiet as he walked Glenda back to Phillip's.

"I'm ruined," he said despondently.

"Why don't you ask Phillip to help out?" suggested Glenda. "I'm sure he's very musical."

"I'm definitely ruined!"

A week later, the evening of the *Stringburrow's* gig dawned, or set, or whatever it was evenings did. For years to come, people would say, "I was there," or at least Gordon hoped they would. He sat in the dressing room backstage, listening to the audience chanting, "Gordon! Gordon! We want Gordon!"

"There's nothing quite like the sound of adoring fans, is there?" he mused quietly, mesmerised by the sound. He hardly even noticed the Gophertones, (who would have given anything for even a couple of adoring fans), shuffling about uneasily, glaring at each other. They weren't talking, which was only marginally better than listening to them arguing.

"They had Shakin' Squirrel here last week," said Glenda, attempting to make conversation and failing.

Spider looked as if he was going to say something, but before he could, there was a knock at the door. The nightclub manager, a well dressed

guinea pig, looked into the room. "You're on!" he said.

"This is it," cried Gordon. "*Top of the Pops,* here we come!" He checked himself out in the mirror, slicked back a stray lick of fur, which wasn't really out of place, but it looked cool, turned up the collar on his biker's jacket and picked up his guitar. He headed for the stage with Glenda. The Gophertones jostled each other in the corridor behind them.

The Gophertones went on stage first to a roar from the audience. Glenda took up her position, then Gordon bounced out into the spotlight to a deafening cheer.

"Good evening, *Stringburrow's!*" he shouted into the mike. "Let's gopher it!"

Another roar went up from the audience.

"One, choo, free, four — hit it!"

Gordon and the Gophertones launched into *Burrow On Down.*

"You all know me, I'm Gordon Gopher.
I'm on TV between two sofas,
I burrow on down..."

"Down, down!" sang Glenda. "He burrows on down!"

The stage lights flashed, the dry ice flowed and the temperature rose. The audience loved it. "Encore! Encore!" they cried as the last notes died away.

Encore? Gordon had forgotten about encores. He only had one song and the Gophertones were getting edgy. What was he going to do? Well, before he could decide, the audience began to storm the stage.

"Oh no, ngmmpg mgff," cried Gordon as he disappeared under a mass of adoring gopher groupies. The Gophertones watched sullenly for a few seconds, then walked off stage in disgust because nobody had bothered to mob them. Spider blamed it on Mick, Mick blamed Gaz, who decided to complain about Spider's drumming drowning out his saxophone, and another argument broke out.

While the Gophertones were busy splitting up, Gordon had managed to escape and make a dash for the safety of the dressing room. He ran in and slammed the door behind him. He leant against it, panting.

"Gordon!" exclaimed Glenda, when she saw him. He had lost one jacket sleeve completely, the other one was hanging off and his face was covered with lipsticky kisses.

"Nobody ever told me that being a pop star was going to be so dangerous!" he said, collapsing into a chair. "I think maybe I'll stick to television in future. I'll last longer that way."

Glenda, for one, was glad to hear it. So was Phillip.

The electric guitar went back into the toy box, Gordon and the Gophertones went down as a footnote in the annals of rock history, and Gordon found plenty of other things to do. But every so often he'd get the guitar out, run through a few riffs and wonder if he shouldn't make a comeback.

Perhaps.
One day.

ELECTION TRAIL

Dateline: Westminster
The next Animal Election is about to take place.
Only you can decide who is going to form the next
government in the Burrow of Commons...

INSTRUCTIONS

- A game for 2 – 4 players.
- You will need counters and a dice.
- Throw a six to start your political campaign
  from your party headquarters.
- If you land on a red square you *gain* votes, so if
  you gain 2 votes, you move forward 2 squares.
- If you land on a blue square you *lose* votes, so
  if you lose 2 votes, you move back 2 squares.
- You must travel *up* the *opinion polls*.
- You must travel *down* the *swingometers*.
- You must throw an exact number to finish, ie if
  you are on square 46, you need to throw a 3 to
  win. If you throw a 4 or over you cannot move.

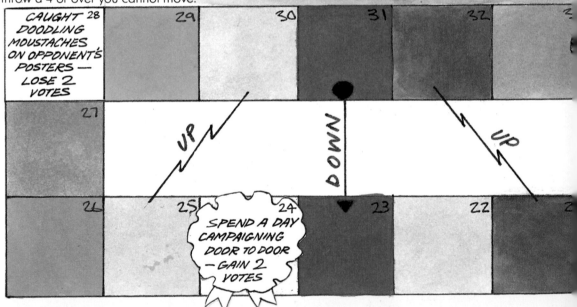

CAUGHT 28 DOODLING MOUSTACHES ON OPPONENT'S POSTERS — LOSE 2 VOTES

29   30   31   32

27

UP   DOWN   UP

26   25   24   23   22

SPEND A DAY CAMPAIGNING DOOR TO DOOR — GAIN 2 VOTES

START

GOPHER H.Q.

1   2   3   4

WOODLAND HEDGEROW ALLIANCE H.Q.

POPULAR MOLEFRONT H.Q.

DOMESTICATED DEMOCRATIC PETS H.Q.

22

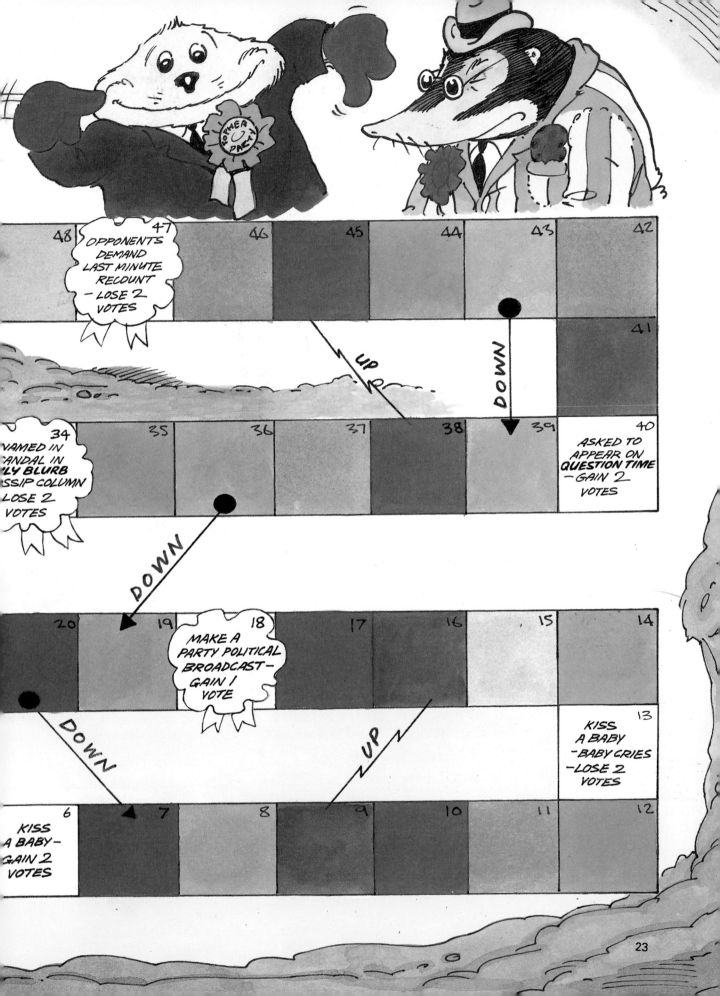

Home on the Prairies

MAURICE MOLE HAD CRAMP. He'd been sitting in the suitcase for about eight hours now and the novelty was wearing thin. It was only the thought of revenge that stopped him from climbing out and going home. That and the fact that he was 35,000 feet up in the cargo hold of a jumbo jet.

A few days earlier he had heard that Gordon and Glenda were flying out to visit Gordon's family in Central America. Maurice fumed. Did Gordon think he could just fly off and leave him slaving away over a hot sink in the BBC canteen? Huh, no chance! Washing up day after day had already affected his paws. They were not only cleaner than they had ever been, they were now softer and fluffier, too. Unfortunately Maurice, being a mole, needed hard, rough paws with which to dig. Now

every time he tried to tunnel he got blisters. Of course, he blamed Gordon and wanted revenge.

Which is why he was now a stowaway on a plane somewhere over Central America. He thought of Gordon sitting above, enjoying his flight, and added another item to his mental list of Things He Had Against Gordon.

In fact Gordon wasn't enjoying his flight that much. He didn't like heights and didn't much care for flying. If gophers were supposed to like heights, reasoned Gordon, they'd be a good deal taller than eighteen inches, and wouldn't have this uncontrollable urge to burrow underground.

Glenda, on the other hand, was thoroughly enjoying the journey. "Oh Gordon, look at the clouds!"

Gordon shook his head. It wasn't so much the

clouds that bothered him, it was the little glimpses of land between them far, far below. He was relieved to hear the captain's voice over the tannoy.

"Please fasten your seat belts. We will be landing at Buenos Prairies Airport shortly. Thank you."

When they landed, Cousin Pablo was waiting for them.

"Cousin Gordon, you arrive, yes?" he cried, crushing Gordon to him in a bearhug. It was a family tradition to greet Gordon this way because he had always been a practical joker and if you shook his hand, he usually used a hand-buzzer that gave you a little shock. While Gordon got his breath back, Pablo bowed to Glenda and kissed her paw. Glenda giggled.

"Glenda," wheezed Gordon, "meet Cousin Pablo."

"Delighted," she said as Pablo picked up her baggage and escorted them to the family truck. It was just as Gordon remembered it, old and dirty and held together by rust, except that now it had the words 'El Cactus Juice Company' painted on the doors. They got in and after a prayer and a bump-start they drove off.

In the airport terminal, Maurice's suitcase (with Maurice inside it) had gone round on the baggage carousel so often that the security guards were getting worried. Mumbling, "Security risk," and tapping their noses knowingly, they took it out onto the tarmac. Then they blew it up in a controlled explosion, "Just to be on the safe side."

Maurice staggered away under cover of the smoke, dazed and slightly crispy round the edges. In his mental notebook of Things He Had Against Gordon he had to turn over and start a new page.

Meanwhile, the Gopher family truck bounced along the pot-holed dirt road that ran through the prairie. Gordon took a deep breath. He could smell the subtle bouquet of the cactus blooms and the sweet fragrance of the prairie. *"Graa-a-atchooo!"*

Prairie grass.

Glenda rummaged in her handbag and produced a handful of crumpled tissues. Gordon snatched at them and managed to stifle a second sneeze, more by luck than judgement.

"Prairie grass," he sniffled. "It's brought on my... my... *atchooo!*...hay fever." He wished Phillip was there. Phillip had a way with tissues when you had hay fever.

They drove on through the prairie, past lots of small cactus plantations where hard working gophers stopped and waved. Pablo tooted the horn in return.

"You see," said Pablo to Gordon, "your idea for the cactus juice business saved all these families. Now we buy all the juice they can collect and sell it all over the world!"

Gordon went a funny colour and tears welled up in his eyes, but that was probably just the hay fever.

They were nearly home. Pablo drove up to the hill where Gordon's family had lived for generations. Because it was under a hill, theirs was the only burrow on the prairie to have windows. For most gophers, windows were just a pipe dream. They would often spend long winter evenings poring wistfully over a pile of double glazing catalogues in much the same way that people do with holiday brochures.

When they pulled up outside the burrow entrance, Gordon saw Aunt Agatha and Uncle Harry waiting on the verandah. As he got out of the truck, Aunt Agatha rushed over and gave him a big hug. Gordon hugged back.

"My, how you've grown, Gordon!" she gasped.

Uncle Harry ambled up and shook Gordon's paw firmly.

"Yeeeow!" yelped Gordon.

"Gotcha, you young rascal!" laughed Uncle Harry, revealing a hand-buzzer in his palm. "I've been waiting for years to do that."

Laughing, Gordon introduced Glenda to his family.

"My!" said Aunt Agatha, looking at her. "So skinny!" She took Glenda indoors. "First you can unpack, dear, then we'll get some good, old-fashioned home cooking inside you."

Cousin Pablo, Uncle Harry and Gordon followed them in with the bags.

At the airport, Maurice had been lurking in the car park. He wanted to skulk, but it seemed faintly ridiculous to skulk in broad daylight wearing a panama hat, Hawaiian shirt, Bermuda shorts and sunglasses. He lurked for a little while longer, throwing in the odd furtive snoop or two, just to keep his hand in, before coming across a solitary bicycle. It was just his size. He looked around. There was nobody else about, so he hopped on and began to pedal as fast as he could in a prairie-wise direction.

Aunt Agatha and Uncle Harry had lived on the prairie all their lives and Gordon was glad to see that the success of the 'El Cactus Juice Company' hadn't changed them one bit. Oh, Uncle Harry had bought a secondhand black and white TV with an indoor aerial, but being underground, the reception was awful. That and Gordon's weekly letters were the only experience they had of the Big Wide World. It seemed a very funny place to them, so they let Cousin Pablo do all the travelling and take care of all the business, as he seemed to like that sort of thing. Even so, they were a little bewildered when Pablo introduced modern production methods into the making of cactus juice.

"I remember taking you cactus tapping when you were little, Gordon," sighed Aunt Agatha, as they all sat chatting after a lunch of home made alfalfa enchilladas. "It's all changed now. You ask Cousin Pablo."

Pablo said he'd show Gordon and Glenda instead. He took them down a long passage that went out under the prairie. It opened out into a huge gopher-made cavern.

"Wow!" said Gordon.

A maze of pipes ran along the roof, little taps were dotted along their length, and at intervals small pipes ran up into the ground above. The floor was divided into aisles by large vats and conveyor belts and stocks of bottled cactus juice. The whole cavern was filled with a sound like ravenous tummy gurgles or somebody sucking the last of the orange squash from a drink carton in a quiet cinema. Only a lot louder.

"It's absolutely mega!" gasped Glenda.

Pablo explained that they were tapping the cactus juice from underneath, so as to preserve the natural environment. After that the words got longer and Gordon lost interest and wandered off. Some moments later Pablo and Glenda were interrupted by a squeal. It was Gordon. He'd been twiddling a valve on a pipe to see what would happen and was now covered in cactus juice.

"Hmmm, 1987, I think," he said, smacking his lips. "Was that a good year?"

"Oh, Gordon!" scolded Glenda.

By now Maurice had reached the prairie. He was in a foul mood. The bumping, bouncing and bruising he received as he rode along the dirt road had left him stiff and sore, and the list of Things He Had Against Gordon had grown by at least half a page as a result. He threw the bicycle down and crept towards the hill.

After much protesting, Gordon finally got into the bath to wash the sticky cactus juice out of his fur. In the kitchen afterwards, Aunt Agatha checked to see if he'd dried his fur properly.

"Atchooo!" sneezed Gordon.

"See! Now your cousin has a cold!" said Aunt Agatha to Pablo. "I knew that city slicker tek-no-ology down there was a bad idea!"

"It's only my hay fever, Aunt," sniffed Gordon.

"But technology is the future, isn't it?" said Glenda.

"Not in Aunt Agatha's book it isn't," Uncle Harry explained.

"This is the future!" declared Cousin Pablo, producing a piece of paper with a flourish.

"What? Cactus juice scented note paper?" said Gordon.

"Ha, ha, ha! Cousin Gordon, always making the jokes," laughed Pablo. "No. This is the secret formula for New Super Fizzy Bubble-Busy Cactusade! I invented it only last week." Pablo slapped the paper down on the kitchen table for everyone to see.

"A-aa-a-atchooo!" Gordon sneezed and blew the formula out of the kitchen window. "Whoops!" he said.

Crouching under the kitchen window, Maurice Mole was surprised and delighted to hear about the formula. If he could get hold of it, he could sell it to a rival soft drinks manufacturer. The 'El Cactus Juice Company' would be ruined.

He was even more surprised and delighted when the formula drifted into his hands without him having to do anything devious to get it. Without a thought to his stiff legs, he raced away across the prairie, chuckling to himself.

"It's Maurice Mole. He's got the formula!" exclaimed Gordon, looking out of the kitchen window. "How on earth did he get here?"

"Stop him!" cried Pablo.

Gordon and Glenda jumped into action. Gordon had been the 400 Metres Shallow Burrowing Champion at Gordonstoun and Glenda was no slouch in that department herself. They burrowed after the mole.

Maurice could see the spot where he had left the bicycle.

"Nearly there," he gasped, but Gordon and Glenda popped up in front of him. Maurice had the sudden feeling that everything was about to go drastically wrong. He was right. He turned to run the other way, but there was a blood-curdling yell and Glenda pounced on him, wrestling him to the ground.

Maurice was stunned.

Gordon was amazed.

"Self defence classes," explained Glenda, sitting on Maurice while Gordon grabbed the formula.

At that moment a police car pulled up and out spilled the Buenos Prairies police captain, the chief of airport security, a customs officer, and a small gopher with an electric guitar who worked part time at the airport, scaring birds off the runway. It was his bike Maurice had stolen.

"That's him," said the customs officer, pointing at Maurice. "He's wanted for illegal immigration, smuggling himself, flying without paying and taking and pedalling away."

Maurice was taken back to the airport and deported immediately, while Gordon and Glenda returned home with the formula.

That evening on the prairie there was a party to celebrate the first batch of New Super Fizzy Bubble-Busy Cactusade.

Everybody, including Aunt Agatha, thought it was wonderful stuff, although she did complain that the bubbles kept going up her nose.

THE *best dressed* GOPHER *IN BRITAIN*

Gordon has won the Best Dressed Gopher in Britain award for two years now. Gordon likes bright colours and says he dresses for comfort. Although he likes shorts and T-shirts, being a TV personality means having an extensive wardrobe for all sorts of occasions. Here, Gordon models some of his present favourites.

How would you like Gordon to slide round to your home plate in this? Cool, huh?

No worries about designer stubble here. Designer fur is in - and how!

Whooo! Mean and moody.

Does this gopher have style, or does this gopher have style?

I TAUGHT HIM
EVERYTHING HE KNOWS!
Phillip

Don't you beleeve it. I'm a natchural. I look good in whatever I ware.

Lookin' good, keepin' fit.

GORDON'S STRIP CARTOONS

make a
GORDON
BADGE

You will need:

thin white card
non-toxic glue
scissors
ruler

sticky tape
felt tip pens
safety pins
paint

pencil
compasses
tracing paper

1. Trace the drawing of Gordon's head on some thin card.
2. Colour it in using felt tip pens or paints.
3. Carefully cut it out. If you used paint, wait until it is dry first.
4. Attach a safety pin to the back of the badge with a piece of sticky tape.

For a Deluxe Gordon Badge use some fur fabric like this:

1. Trace the outline of Gordon's head on some thin card.
2. Cut it out.
3. Use the card as a stencil and on the <u>back</u> of a piece of fur fabric draw round it.
4. Cut out the fur fabric shape.
5. Glue onto thin card.
6. Trace the outline of the eyes, nose and mouth onto thin card, and colour in.
7. Cut them out and carefully glue them into place on the fur fabric.
8. Attach a safety pin to the back of the badge with sticky tape.

more GORDON BADGES

Why not try making a badge with an authorised gopher slogan?

1. Using compasses, draw a circle with a diameter of about 5cm on thin card. It doesn't even have to be a circle; it could be square or rectangular.
2. Carefully add the slogan of your choice.
3. With sticky tape, attach a safety pin to the back of the badge.

SLOGANS

Here are some suggestions — or why not make up your own?

GOPHER-IT!

I ♥ GORDON

BURROW ON DOWN!

QUOTE GOPHER

I VOTED X GOPHER PARTY

GORDON AND THE GOPHERTONES!

THE CHUNNEL AFFAIR

SOMEWHERE UNDER THE Houses of Parliament, but above the MPs' underground car park and off to one side of Westminster tube station is the Burrow of Commons, the hub of animal politics in Britain today. It is here that the Animal Parliament meets to discuss the welfare of British wildlife.

On one side of the Burrow sits the Gopher Party, who have held power since the 1987 Animal General Election. Sitting in rowdy rows on the opposition side are representatives of the Woodlands and Hedgerows Alliance, the Domesticated Democratic Pets Party, and somewhere over in the far corner, near the fire exit

and next to the broom cupboard, sits Maurice Mole, the only member of the Popular Mole Front to get himself re-elected.

Maurice Mole had been having a bad time of it recently. His new business venture, an underground theme park called *Mole World,* was proving a dismal failure. Whether this was because his advertising budget was restricted to one small advert in the *Shepherd's Hedge Advertiser,* or the fact that the only entrance to *Mole World* was a disused pit shaft, it was hard to say. Nevertheless, it left Maurice in a bad mood and he had decided to take it out on someone. Someone cute, furry, well-known and successful, namely Gordon the Gopher. Maurice had come up with a really devious plan to ruin Gordon's political career. Even more devious than the last one.

It was because of this plan that the Burrow of Commons was presently in uproar. Maurice had been stirring up trouble and had put Gordon on the spot.

"Awda, awda!" cried the Squeaker of the Burrow of Commons, banging his gavel down and mashing his banana and sesame seed sandwich by accident.

The noise slowly subsided and all eyes turned to Maurice Mole.

"My Right Honorable Gopher," he began, which given the circumstances, sounded quite polite for Maurice, but it was only proper parliamentary talk, and he wasn't allowed to call Gordon anything else, even if he wanted to, which he did. "My Right

Honourable Gopher still hasn't answered the question. What does he intend doing about this...this Eurotunnel thing? It's an outrage! Here we are, the most powerful group of burrowing animals in the country, and we weren't even consulted. They went right over our heads on this!"

"Don't you mean under our feet?" said Gordon from the Gopher Party bench.

"Whatever," Maurice continued, glaring at him. "So what do you intend to do about it? We want an answer!"

"Hear, hear!" cried various animals from the opposition benches. "An answer, an answer, we want an answer!"

"Awda!"

The cries died down to a discontented murmur as the Burrow waited to hear what Gordon would say.

"Ahem!" Gordon cleared his throat. "My Right Honourable Members. That's cool. I can relate to that, no problem. So listen, here's what I'm going to do, okay? The way I see it is this..."

"Get on with it!" jeered a weasel from the back benches.

"I'll write a letter to the Prime Minister," said Gordon. "A strong letter. A strong letter with big words."

An 'oooh' of admiration arose from a few of the younger animals.

Encouraged, Gordon went on. "And I'll hold a press conference."

"But they won't be able to understand what you

say, Gordon," piped up a hedgehog from the Woodlands and Hedgerows Alliance.

"Er...okay then, I'll issue a press release. That's it, I'll issue a press release."

There was a general murmur of grudging acceptance, and with that the Eurotunnel question was settled for the moment. The Burrow then moved on to more pressing business. Maurice sat back and gloated quietly to himself for the rest of the afternoon. Phase one of his masterplan was complete.

After a hard day's parliamenting, Gordon trudged over to the Gopher Party offices at Whitehole, under Whitehall, to consult with a fellow gopher — the Minister for Underground Affairs — on this Eurotunnel problem.

"Hrmph!" coughed the minister thoughtfully when Gordon had filled him in on the day's proceedings. "This Eurotunnel thing. It sounds like a political hot potato!"

"It does?" said Gordon.

"Handle it with kid gloves."

"Don't you mean oven gloves? I mean if it's a hot potato..."

"I mean it's a potentially explosive affair."

"It is?"

"If mishandled, you could end up with egg on your face."

"I thought you said it was a potato?" said Gordon.

"Tread carefully. It's obviously a very sensitive subject in the Burrow. Make a bad job of it and they could return a vote of no confidence in you, you'll be out on your political ear, and they'll hold another election!"

"Crumbs!" said Gordon, and he went straight home to draft a letter to the Prime Minister and draw up a press release for the newspapers.

Because of his handwriting, it took quite some time before he managed to produce something even halfway legible, that is, if you discounted the odd paw print, ink blot and numerous spelling mistakes.

"There, that ought to do it," said Gordon, adding his signature in rather wobbly joined-up writing. He sent the letter round to the Prime Minister and rushed the press release round to the newspapers so that they could print it the next day.

He was a little worried the next morning when

he couldn't find any mention of his press release on the front page of his newspaper, but eventually he found it at the bottom of page five. It couldn't have been harder to find if it wasn't there at all. And there was nothing from the Prime Minister in the post, either. "Uh oh!" said Gordon, feeling a vote of no confidence coming on.

When the bell went for the start of proceedings at the Burrow of Commons that morning, Maurice Mole was the first to speak. Waving a copy of that morning's paper in one paw and brandishing a magnifying glass in the other, he stood up.

"This isn't good enough!" he boomed. "The time for words has obviously passed. We need more than words. We need *action!* If this Eurotunnel digging is allowed to continue, it will be very bad for the morale of the British animal. Think of it — all the digging done by machine!"

"Hear, hear! Action, action! Picket the tunnel!" The Burrow of Commons was in uproar again. Maurice Mole sat down with a self-satisfied smirk. For once he wouldn't like to be in Gordon's shoes.

For his part, Gordon had the distinct feeling that things were getting a little out of paw. There was nothing he could do but put on the proverbial oven gloves and grip the political hot potato with both hands.

"Very well," he squeaked, "I'll lead a picket to the Eurotunnel tomorrow!"

"Hear, hear! Good show! I should think so too!"

The Squeaker of the Burrow of Commons excused everybody for the rest of the day and they all started making placards to take with them on the picket.

The picket proved less than successful. The Eurotunnel site was muddy, noisy, and full of huge machines trundling about. A bunch of cold, wet and miserable animals led by Gordon, walking round in circles, holding placards, didn't cause much disruption or attract much attention. Except for a particularly exciting ten minutes when a TV camera crew turned up to film their protest for the news.

That evening, in his burrow, Gordon watched the news as he had never watched it before. He was bitterly disappointed to find that the piece about their protest was broadcast as a novelty item at the end, just after a story about a chihuahua who could play the piano.

"That's it. I'm doomed. My political career is over.

Down the tubes. Kaput. I'm history," he said despondently, convinced that nothing would stop the Burrow of Commons passing a vote of no confidence in him now.

Maurice, on the other hand, was chuckling with delight. It looked as if Gordon was going to have a very hard time at the Burrow the next day. There remained only one thing to do. It had come to him while watching the news report — a way of ensuring Gordon's political fate and saving *Mole World*. The combination was too great to resist.

Later that night, Maurice called together the members of the S.A.S. (the Subterranean Anti-gopher Squad), which consisted of himself and a couple of like-minded moles who just happened to own balaclavas.

After kitting themselves out with spanners, screwdrivers, maps, compasses and the odd chocolate-covered worm bar to keep them going, they burrowed down to the site of the Eurotunnel. Once there, they began to tamper with the huge drilling machines.

One veered off and started tunnelling towards Spain instead of France, and the other doubled back on itself and started digging back towards England. Towards *Mole World,* to be precise. It was Maurice's plan to divert the Eurotunnel trains so that they ended up at *Mole World* and lots of people would have to pay exorbitant prices in order to leave. It couldn't fail.

But how did all this affect Gordon? The answer came with the morning papers. 'Sabotage' screamed the headlines, and articles drew connections between Gordon's anti-Eurotunnel protest of the previous day and the night's sabotage of the drilling machines. Was Gordon involved? It was too much of a coincidence, they said. Rumours flew around like custard pies. Even though none of it was true, the scandal wouldn't help Gordon's political career one little bit.

But Gordon hadn't seen the morning papers. He'd got a letter from the Prime Minister saying that they had made a mistake in not approaching the Burrow of Commons about the Eurotunnel project

and would they please consider forming an independent working party of burrowing animals to act as consultants on the project?

"Hot diggetty dig!" exclaimed Gordon. "I'm saved!" and he was too excited to even eat his breakfast, let alone read the paper. He didn't even bother looking at the cartoons. He rushed straight off to the Burrow of Commons with the letter.

When he arrived, the place was in uproar. Again.

He was met by the Minister for Underground Affairs. "Have you heard the news?" the minister asked urgently.

"Yeah! I got the letter this morning. Mega, isn't it?" replied Gordon.

"What letter? I'm talking about the newspapers,

Gordon explained about the letter and the minister told him about the sabotage and the rumours. They were just wondering what on earth they were going to do when the news came through.

Apparently, the Eurotunnel workmen had finally caught up with the runaway drilling machines, where they found carelessly discarded chocolate-covered worm bar wrappers and realised that one of the machines was boring its way to *Mole World*. When they put two and two together, they knew Gordon was innocent. Everybody knew that Gordon was a vegetarian, and would have been public spirited enough to throw his litter in a bin anyway.

All the evidence pointed towards Maurice Mole as the guilty party, but he had gone underground as soon as the news broke and nobody could find him.

At the Burrow of Commons, the animals soon began to realise that it was Maurice who had brought up the Eurotunnel question in the first place, dropping Gordon in it, so moments later, when Gordon entered the chamber, he was greeted by a loud cheer. Everybody had heard the news about his innocence. There was an even louder cheer and a standing ovation when Gordon told them about the letter, which everybody thought was cause for a celebration. The Squeaker of the Burrow of Commons abandoned the day's proceedings and they all went off and had a jolly good party instead, which pleased Gordon no end.

"This is the kind of political party I like best!" he said.

BURROW ON DOWN

by
G.T. Gopher

You all know me, I'm Gordon Gopher.
I'm on TV between two sofas.
Burrow on down (down down)
(Burrow on down).

I'm a gopher 'cos I like diggin'.
You like it too? Well, come on - join in.
We'll burrow on down (down down)
(We'll burrow on down).

CHORUS
Don't get sad or hoppin' mad or cry
   or frown,
Just burrow on down.

We'll have a party in my burrow.
You gotta friend? Well they can
   come too.
So burrow on down (down down)
(So burrow on down).

The music's loud, the party's swingin'.
Who's at the door? Phillip? Well
   come in.

Burrow on down (down down)
(Burrow on down).

CHORUS
Don't get sad or hoppin' mad or cry
   or frown,
Just burrow on down.

So listen here, we gotta secret.
You wanna be cool, wanna be hip?
Burrow on down (down down)
(Burrow on down).

CHORUS
Don't get sad or hoppin' mad or cry
   or frown,
Gopher it,
Just burrow on down.

(Burrow on down down down)
(Burrow on down).

fade

SQUEAK MAGAZINE

CELEBRITY INTERVIEW GORDON T. GOPHER FAME AND FUR (TUNE)

Who is this Cool Dude, this Hoopy Frood? This Bruce Willis of the Shepherd's Hedge Set? Where did he come from? And why? And will live television ever be the same again?

We sent the Ever Hip Hal Hamster, *Squeak Magazine*'s very own Cool Dude, to find out…

Shepherd's Hedge. Not exactly the kind of place you'd expect to find a celebrity, and not exactly the kind of place you'd go to find one, either. Still, that was the address on the piece of paper the Editor gave me. "Go to it!" he said. So here I am. At it. But what the hey, I'm hip. I press the front door bell to his burrow. It plays the first three bars of *Burrow On Down*. The Main Gopher himself answers the door. Funny really, he looks bigger on the telly. He invites me in to this amazing, untidy, open plan, split level (this effect I later find out is due to subsidence as opposed to trendy architectural planning) bachelor pad. It's so cool it practically has icicles hanging from the ceiling! He kicks a few stray toys nonchalantly behind the sofa and offers me a seat, giggling.

THRRRRRP! That's right. A whoopee cushion. How did you guess? After he has stopped laughing and dried the tears from his face, he breaks out the cactus juice (the family label, don't you know) and we get down to some serious rapping…

41

So, Gordon T. Gopher, what does the 'T' stand for?

I don't know. What does the 'T' stand for?

You tell me.

Oh, sorry, I thought you were going to tell me a joke for a minute there. You know, to break the ice. Well actually, most people think it stands for 'The' as in 'Gordon The Gopher'. I mean it can do, but it doesn't.

EMBARRASSING

So what does it stand for then?

Anything embarrassing?

Well, you know, it's a family tradition kind of thing. Passed on down the generations.

So it does stand for something embarrassing then?

(Silence)

Okay. What did you want to be when you were little?

Taller (laughs).

You grew up on the prairie, didn't you? Did you have any ambitions when you were younger?

No, but I did have a pet rock called Herbert. We were inseparable. I used to spend a lot of time teaching him little tricks. He could play dead and stay better than any other rock I know. They said that pet rocks were a great responsibility, what with the house training and everything. They said he would be a millstone around my neck, but he wasn't 'cos I used to carry him in my pocket. It was my dearest wish to see Herbert grow up into a young boulder, get a good education and a nice job as an apprentice mountain or something.

HERBERT

So what happened? Where's Herbert now?

Well one day I took him down to the brook. I thought I'd teach him how to swim and...well, I don't like to talk about it.

Do you come from a big family?

No, I wouldn't say so. We're all under sixty centimetres as a rule (laughs). Yes, actually I do. We all lived under a hill on the prairie, about forty kilometres from Buenos Prairies.

In which direction?

I'm not telling. Anyway, I used to live there with Mum, Dad, my brothers, sisters, aunties, uncles, cousins, in-laws. You name them, they lived there. It was quite a busy little hill.

FORTUNE

And what was it that made you decide to leave the prairie and seek your fortune?

It was my cousin, Pablo. Definitely. He's older than me. We used to sit on top of the hill in the evening and look out over the prairie to the mountains on the horizon, and I'd wonder what lay beyond them. Cousin Pablo used to tell me fantastic tales of the Big Wide World Beyond the Prairie. It just got to the stage where one day I had to go and see for myself. So one day, shortly after Herbert's ill-fated swimming lesson, I packed a rucksack, said goodbye to my family and set off to see the Big Wide World. It was only when I got there that I realised that Cousin Pablo had made up all his stories to amuse me, but by then it was too late, and I was on a ship full of car parts bound for Britain.

You must have had some pretty wild adventures with all this travelling about — crossing the prairie, trekking through Central America, sailing the seas...

Yes.

Aren't you going to talk about it?

Well, no, I don't think so. You see, I'm planning on writing my autobiography one day and I've a feeling I'm going to need all the anecdotes I can find!

Staying on the subject of clothes for a moment, you've been voted Best Dressed Gopher in Britain. What's your secret?

Not trying. If you haven't got it — forget it!

But if you don't try, how will you ever know if you've got it or not?

Aha! That's the secret!

What are your favourite fashion colours?

I don't really have any favourite colours. I like my clothes bright and jazzy, and if they happen to clash with whatever Phillip's wearing, so much the better (laughs).

PABLO

Do you still keep in touch with your family?

Oh yes. Cousin Pablo is now running a very profitable cactus juice business which employs most of the family and quite a few other local gophers besides. With the profits, Mum and Dad have bought a caravan and are currently touring North America with my brothers and sisters, getting to see the Big Wide World at last. Very few of my family have ever travelled beyond the prairie. And of course I write every week, let the kinfolk know how I'm getting on and post my dirty laundry home to be washed — that sort of thing! (Laughs). No, I'm only joking. I go to the launderette down the road.

You do your own laundry then?

I used to, until the day I slipped and fell into the washing machine. I was well into second rinse before I was rescued. Now I pay a little extra and the nice lady at the launderette does it all for me.

I just thought I'd sneak this in while Gordon wasn't looking. It's his old school report. I found it at the bottom of a drawer. No wonder he tried to hide it!

GORDONSTOUN PUBLIC SCHOOL
(GECO Placement Scheme)

SCHOOL REPORT

Name: GORDON T. GOPHER
Class: Lower 1st
Copies: School Files/Pupil/Gopher Education Concern Organization

SUBJECT	MARKS	
DRAMA	B+	Good! Confident, Natural talent and Charisma. A career in T.V. perhaps? J.k
ENGLISH	C	Average. P.B.
GOPHEREESE	A+	Quite Outstanding! S.T.G.
HANDWRITING	D –	Poor. Enthusiastic but inept. Should stick to using pencil and stay away from ink for everyone's sake. P.H.
MATHS	C	Can do better. Should pay more attention in class. B.C.
MINE ENGINEERING	A+	Excellent. His grasp of the practical aspects of Tunnelling is very good. Keep it up. M.W.
POLITICS	B	Promising. Interesting economic theories. I feel he could make Prime Minister one day. E.M.
SPELLING	D+	Weak. At least, I think it's weak. I can't read most of it. PT
SPORT	B –	Enthusiastic, but must learn to jump over hurdles instead of burrowing under them. G.R.

GENERAL PROGRESS

An easy going, confident young gopher and much liked. He has learnt a lot while he has been here and could go far, if he wasn't so inattentive and given to playing pratical jokes. A pity about his handwriting and spelling.

C. J. Grunion.   Head of Placement Year.

The Gordonstoun Ghost

URMURS WERE HEARD IN concerned quarters. They were agreed with, nodded at, and finally acted upon. The first Gordon knew of all this was when the letter came through his door.

It was a very official-looking envelope with a little window in the front and an 'if undelivered please return to' address on the back. He opened it. The letter was from GECO, the Gopher Education Concern Organization. Their files showed (the letter said) that Gordon had not fulfilled the required amount of education for a gopher in the UK which (under the present administration) was nine weeks. He was instructed to choose a school from the list (enclosed) and attend. They didn't say what would happen if he didn't, and Gordon was quite sure he didn't want to find out. He looked glumly at the list and the name of one school leapt out at him saying, "Choose me!", only not in so many words. The name of the school was Gordonstoun. He filled in the form (attached) and sent it off (in the pre-paid envelope provided).

Within a month Gordon found himself at Gordonstoun with two other gophers, Grenville and Gareth, who were also on their GECO placements.

It was a busy, famous old school that seemed to be full of lesson bells and corridors, no end of pupils rushing about trying to get to lessons, and even more pupils dawdling, trying to avoid them. The air was filled with the smell of ancient chalk dust, bungled chemistry experiments and the aroma of boiled cabbage and gravy from the school kitchens. It was just as Gordon imagined it would be, right down to the hard toilet paper.

Gordon hardly had time to learn how to tie his school tie before finding himself knee deep in twice nineteens, algebras, nouns, adverbs, 1812s, 1066s and European Wheat Production. It was all very bewildering stuff.

There were one or two things he really got to grips with, though. One was mine engineering, which taught you all about the scientific side of digging. Until then, Gordon hadn't even realised

there was one — he just stuck his paws in the ground and it just sort of happened. The other thing he enjoyed was sports, especially the 400 Metres Shallow Burrowing and the Freestyle Excavating, although he wasn't too keen on the early morning Cross Country Burrowing, not least because it was before breakfast — and that was at 7.30!

Gradually Gordon settled into the school routine and began to make friends. He even joined the Junior Fire Service which the school ran two times a week and once at weekends.

The only person he didn't really get on with was Wimpkins Major, who was his house prefect and had a room opposite the gophers' dorm. Gordon did try, but apparently Wimpkins had got his head stuck in a rabbit hole or something when he was little and had grown up with an aversion to all things cute and furry and burrowing as a result. Well, that's what Grenville said, anyway.

One day, after a trying afternoon in triple handwriting, a very inky Gordon trudged dismally back to the dorm, having completely failed to master a particularly squiggly kind of letter t. When he got there, he found Grenville and Gareth waiting impatiently for him. They seemed excited.

"Gordon, Gordon. Look!" squeaked Grenville.

Gordon looked. There by his bed was a wicker hamper, all tied up and with a little note attached. Gordon immediately cheered up. He let out a whoop of delight, bounced off his bed and landed right next to the hamper. Grenville and Gareth crowded round as much as two small gophers could.

"What is it? What does the note say? Who's it from?" they asked eagerly.

Gordon detached the little note.

"It's from Phillip," he said. "It's a food hamper."

"Ooooh!" said Gareth.

Gordon wasted no time in undoing all the string and opening the hamper to reveal a grade 'A' midnight feast. But that wasn't all. Underneath a false bottom was a smuggled supply of soft toilet paper. Good old Phillip.

"Ooooh!" said Grenville.

Just then, the dormitory door swung open. It was Wimpkins Major.

"What's all this then?" he said, spying the open food hamper. Gordon hastily replaced the false bottom. "Planning a midnight feast, are we? Why wasn't I invited? I'll tell you why. 'Cos you're not going to have one! I'm confiscating this hamper right now, so there!" Wimpkins shut the hamper lid and used Gareth's spare chain and padlock, usually used for securing his bike, to lock it up. "I'm doing this for your own good," he sneered. "After all, you don't want to meet the ghost, do you?"

A squeak went up from Grenville.

"That's right," said Wimpkins. "He appears at midnight — the ghost of an ancient fourth former, cursed to wander the school rattling his chains and conjugating French verbs forever! Ha, ha, ha!" And with that he dragged the hamper off and locked it in the cellar.

"Oh well, that's that," said Gareth, hearing the cellar door clang shut.

"He-he said a-a ghost!" stammered Grenville.

"There's no such thing," said Gordon. "My Aunt Agatha says things like that are just the result of eating too much alfalfa rarebit before bedtime."

"Really?" asked Grenville.

"Far as I know," replied Gordon.

"Phew! That's a relief," sighed Grenville, flopping down onto his bed. "So what are we going to do now that old Wimpkins has taken our midnight feast?"

"And our soft toilet paper," added Gordon. "The rotter!"

That night, after lights out, Gordon lay in bed. He couldn't sleep. He could almost hear those goodies in the hamper calling to him. Actually, it was more the other way around. His stomach was gurgling under the bedclothes.

"It's no use," he said, "I'll have to get the hamper back. But how?"

Lying there in bed he got to thinking, and the thinking reached a conclusion, and the conclusion went something like this: *Fact* — GECO had been educating gophers in Britain for decades. *Fact* — some of them must have been to Gordonstoun. *Fact* — Gophers will be gophers. *Therefore* — somewhere under the dormitory there must be a tunnel or burrow that might lead to the cellar. It was a long shot, but his stomach seemed to think it was worth a try, and grumbled in agreement.

Which was why, when Grenville and Gareth woke up in the middle of the night, they found Gordon shuffling round in his PJs, tapping floorboards for all he was worth, listening for that peculiar hollow sort of sound that suggests that there might be a hidden passage there. Grenville and Gareth thought it was a great idea and joined in immediately.

But nobody was more surprised than Gordon when they actually found something. He discovered it under his bed. Loose floorboards.

TAP! TAP!

47

Gareth brought his bicycle lamp and the gophers all crowded under Gordon's bed as he lifted up the floorboards.

"There is a burrow!" he whispered triumphantly.

"Look, there's something scratched on the bottom of that floorboard," said Grenville. "What does it say?"

"Gilbert the Gopher," read Gordon, "and the date — 1921/22."

"Wow!"

There was a moment's silent appreciation for the mysterious Gilbert's engineering skills then one by one, they slipped into the burrow.

Nobody had been down there for years. Dust and cobwebs covered everything. Grenville picked up an old green cactus juice bottle, the kind with a glass marble stopper, the kind they didn't make anymore. Gareth found an old copy of *Home and Burrow* dated October 1936.

"Wow!" said Gordon, playing the beam from the bicycle lamp down three tunnels that led off from the burrow. "These must run right under the whole school!"

"But which one goes to the cellar?" asked Grenville.

"We'll have to try all three!" declared Gordon. "Come on, let's explore."

The first one they tried came up on the other side of the school gate. Useful, but not quite what they were looking for. The second went to the kitchens and branched off under the library and assembly hall.

"It's got to be the last one," said Gordon. "Hasn't it?"

They shuffled down the passage until they came to the end.

"Does this look like the cellar to you?" asked Gordon. "It looks like the cellar to me." Gareth and Grenville had to admit that it looked very much like a cellar. If the hamper was down here, they'd find it. Gordon's stomach let out an experimental rumble. The hamper answered with a faint aroma of alfalfa chip cookies and Gordon's acute sense of smell picked up the trail from there.

It wasn't long before they came across the hamper, tucked away in a dark corner, looking as miserable and dejected as only a wicker hamper in a cellar can.

"At last!" said Gordon, feeling a little like Indiana Jones. Or should that be Prairie Gordon? "Oh no," he added when he saw the padlock and chain.

"Don't worry, I've got a spare key back in the dorm," said Gareth.

"Great, let's get it back to Gilbert's burrow then," said Gordon.

They dragged the hamper into the tunnel, but Gilbert, whoever he was, had never done any hamper smuggling in his day. It was a very tight fit and it kept catching on knobbly bits sticking out of the tunnel wall, and the chain kept getting snagged too. The three gophers pulled and heaved, but it was hard work.

Somewhere above, Wimpkins sat up in bed,

eyes like saucers, ears twitching. The radio alarm by his bed said 00:02. Midnight. He was sure he heard something. Were those cute, furry gophers having a midnight beano? Wait. There it was again, very faint, sort of hollow.

Uggggghhhhh rattle shuffle clank uggghhh!

Wimpkins went as white as a sheet.

"The...the ghost!"

He listened in horror to the sounds until they faded some minutes later. As soon as they had, he was out of bed like a shot. He locked the bedroom door, shot the bolts, barricaded it with his desk, chair and bedside cabinet before creeping back to bed and sleeping fitfully until morning.

Uggghhh!

Rattle. Shuffle.

"Nearly there!" exclaimed Gordon as they emerged into Gilbert's burrow beneath their own dorm. Gareth brought his spare key and in no time at all the hamper was open. Stomachs rumbled impatiently as they tucked into the feast. It was the best midnight feast they had ever had.

There were many more midnight feasts after that because Wimpkins spent every night barricaded inside his room and wouldn't come out again until morning. Gordon never did find out why.

And although he often explored the tunnels under the school he never found out any more about the mysterious Gilbert the Gopher either.

PHILLIP'S FUNNIES

*I couldn't stand another page of Gordon's awful jokes
— so here are some of mine instead... Phillip*

What's green, then red, then green, then red?
A cucumber that works part time as a tomato.

Two fleas were going home after a night out.
"Shall we walk?" said one flea.
"No," said the other, "let's take a dog."

What's locked up and wears a thermos on his head?
The Man in the Iron Flask.

"How big is an elephant?"
"What kind of elephant?"
"A big one."
"How big?"

What goes cluck...cluck...BANG!?
A chicken in a minefield.

What colour are hiccups?
Burple.

Why are elephants wrinkled?
You try and iron one!

Why did the bees go on strike?
They wanted shorter flowers and more honey.

51

Tuesday 5th July

Still no fan mail. Went round to David Attenborough's. He wazn't in. Did stuff. Dead bored.

POW!

SUPER! GOPHER! and PHILLIP THE BOY WONDER

FLICK THEM WITH YOUR HAIR GEL BOY WONDER

Glenda

GG

Take that, Doctor Mauricestein your evil Mole-botz won't take over the world while I'm here.

MY BAFTA AWARD

For Services to Gophers

Wednesday 6th July

Dear Diary, HOORAY!!

My fan mail arrived today. It had been misdirected to Ian McCaskill, the weatherman. I don't look anything like him - do I? Anyway, got tonz more mail than Phillip. He mite az well give up. I wrote to David Attenborough to see if he wantz an assistant ha! ha!

Gud nite dear diary, must cloze now.

Thursday 7th July

✳ MUMS BURTHDAY

Ooops! Dear Diary. Why didn't you remind me? Posted Mum's prezunt. Phillip took me for my anewal booster shot. OUCH! I couldn't sit down for hourz. Zomebody ought to pazz a law against this zort of thing. Get my own back next week - I have to take Phillip to the dentizt.

Friday 8th July

* BATH NITE - ARRANGE TO BE OUT!!!

Dear Diary - you're useless. Posted Mum's buthday card! Late nite debate at Burrow of Commons. Had brainwave. Tried to pass law against booster shots, but the Rite on Minister for Helth and Vetnary Surgery said they were ~~nessesss~~ ~~neieser~~ ~~nessss~~ nessesr had to be done. He wouldn't say that if he saw what I saw in the vet's hand yesterday, I bet!

Saturday 9th July

* LAUNDRY

Dear Diary, wrote powim to Glenda, what do you think? Is your powetic apreeseeashun as bad as your memory?

oh to be in Paris
Now that autumn's here.
All the leaves are falling -
It's that time of year.

They're lying on the pavement
All slushy with the rain,
Except for those who miss the road
And float off down the Seine.

I thort it was dead romantic. Glenda said dead was the word. I wonder what she meant by that. Funny things, girls...

Sunday 10th July

ALFALFA #UNTING ZEAZON OPENS.

Got up late. Wrote a letter to Auntie Agatha and Uncle Harry. After lunch, sined pho

sined fotos of myself until I got writers cramp. Must be careful - it is my burrowing arm! Fan mail tomorrow. Hooray! Gud nite, diary.

GORDON'S STRIP CARTOONS

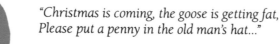

GORDON SAVES CHRISTMAS

*"Christmas is coming, the goose is getting fat,
Please put a penny in the old man's hat..."*

I T WAS CHRISTMAS EVE and the day before Gordon's birthday, the goose was on a diet, the old man (after a particularly successful year on the stock market) was busy putting pennies into other people's hats from the window of his Rolls Royce, and somehow, Gordon the Gopher knew that this wasn't going to be just any sort of ordinary Christmas.

"Gordon, are you listening?" said Phillip as they walked down Oxford Street, arms piled high with last-minute gifts.

"Sorry, Phillip," said Gordon from behind his pile of parcels. "What did you say?"

"I said, I think we ought to be getting back. It's late, my wallet's nearly empty, my credit cards have positively melted through over-use, and besides — my feet are killing me!"

"Suits me," came Gordon's reply as he staggered along under his shopping. "I thought you'd never come out of that store!"

"Me? What about you? You're the one who kept going back to see Santa in his grotto — seventeen times!"

"Well, I lost my list, and kept remembering things I'd forgotten to mention."

"Come on," said Phillip wearily, "let's go home before you remember something else."

So back they went to Phillip's house.

Phillip had invited Gordon to spend Christmas with him. Gordon was delighted, but he didn't like

to think of Santa coming all that way, finding an empty burrow, and not leaving anything because he thought Gordon had moved, so he left a note on the door:

DEER SANTA,
I AM STAYING AT PHILLIP'S.
PLEEZE REEDIREKT ENY PREZUNTS.
THANKEW. MERY KRISMUS. FROM
GORDON

"There was no need to do that, Gordon," said Phillip. "Santa Claus knows where you'll be, just as he knows if you've been good or bad."

"He does? How?" asked Gordon, who was a bit worried, wondering how practical jokes counted on a scale of good to bad.

"Magic!" said Phillip. "He knows everything, so just watch out, young fellow!"

Gordon said he intended to, because he was planning to stake out the stockings that evening and catch Santa in the act. He had his instant camera loaded and waiting, a flask of hot cactus punch to keep him warm, and a little hidey-hole in the corner behind the Christmas tree. He was also going to leave a plate of mince pies on the mantelpiece as bait.

"It's no good," said Phillip. "You won't catch him. 'He knows when you're sleeping, he knows when you're awake', and all that."

But Gordon was determined, and nothing Phillip could do or say would make him budge from behind the tree, so Phillip gave up, went to bed and left him to it.

It wasn't long, however, before Gordon, tired and over-excited, fell asleep himself.

On the last stroke of midnight, looking as if they'd escaped from a Steven Spielberg film, clouds heavy with the promise of snow began to billow out of nowhere, rolling across the slumbering landscape with a deeply melodic, almost magical rumble. For a long while afterwards there was silence, then snow began to fall and, carried on the wind, there came a faint tinkling of bells...sleigh bells.

Ching, ching! Ching, ching! Ching, ching!

"Ho, ho, ho! All right, Rudolph. Take her down."

"Roger. Commencing descent."

A darkened sleigh slipped under the cloud cover over London.

"No, no! Pull up, Rudolph, pull up! You're going to clip the side of that..."

Clang!

"...tower block..."

Some time later Gordon awoke to the sound of urgent whispering.

"I've told you before about those steep descents, Rudolph. If you'd listened, we wouldn't be in this mess!"

"At least I've got my pilot's licence. Honestly, you can be such a back seat driver sometimes, Kris.

Chomp, chomp! Any more of those mince pies left?"

Gordon reached for his instant camera.

Flaaash!

"Wait until Phillip sees this," said Gordon.

"We've been rumbled!" cried Rudolph, with a mouthful of mince pie.

"Hello Gordon," said Santa Claus. "Ho, ho, ho," he added despondently.

Gordon shuffled out from behind the tree.

"If you'll excuse me saying so, Santa, that didn't seem like a particularly jolly ho, ho, ho just then," he said quietly. "Are you feeling a little under the weather? I expect it's all this running around. It can't be healthy."

"No, no, no, it's not that," said Santa. "We've just got a bit of a problem, that's all. I don't suppose you know anything about computers, do you?"

"Computers?"

Santa explained that it wasn't easy keeping up to date files on all the millions of children these days, so he exchanged information with the tooth fairies, who visited them regularly, and the bogeymen, who couldn't keep files for toffee, but knew where all the naughty ones lived.

Recently, however, because of the increased strength of the molar on the international magic exchange, the tooth fairies had invested in a computer and transferred their files to that. To keep up, Santa had to install a mainframe at the North Pole. The elves in filing were over the moon. They could access a child's address, what they wanted for Christmas, and whether they deserved it, all at the touch of a button.

Because of the enormous distances Santa travelled, the sleigh was fitted with an onboard computer and a small satellite dish on the back. The information could then be relayed via an orbiting Santallite which the dish tracked automatically.

Unfortunately Rudolph had clipped a block of flats, knocking the dish out of alignment, and now they had lost the signal.

"That's well depressing," said Gordon sympathetically. He thought hard for a moment. "I know a bit about computers," he added.

"You do? Splendid!" said Santa, clapping his hands. "I'd do it myself, but I haven't got the hang of it yet, and Rudolph is all antlers and hooves when it comes to the fiddly stuff."

Rudolph and Santa took Gordon out to the sleigh and sat him in Santa's seat.

"First I'll need the co-ordy-thingies of the Santallite," he said, paws poised over the keyboard of the little onboard computer. Santa mumbled something that sounded more like a telephone number than a whatsit, but Gordon tapped it in anyway. The computer began humming to itself and before long the answer popped up on the screen. The gears in the satellite dish drive motor ground and whirred but nothing happened, so Gordon clambered over to the back of the sleigh and gave the dish a swift kick. Santa stared at him.

"I have the same problem with my changeformer robot," explained Gordon.

The gears became unstuck, the dish swivelled to look at the stars, and the computer screen burst into life.

"Bravo, young Gordon! Well done. You've saved Christmas! I daren't think what would have happened without you," said Santa, all jolly again.

Gordon smiled, shuffled about awkwardly, and went all red under his fur. "It was nothing, really."

"Come now, Gordon. There must be some way we can show our gratitude?" said Santa kindly.

Gordon immediately thought of at least a dozen things he could add to his presents list, but somehow it didn't seem right to ask for them.

"Do you...do you think I could have a look at *my* file?" he squeaked finally.

"I don't see why not. I'll just — what's the phrase, punch it up?"

Tac tacca tackitty tac!

Gordon's file flashed up in glowing green on the screen. At least it said it was Gordon's file, but Gordon wasn't too sure...

"But..." he began. Santa had obviously made a mistake. Gordon was just wondering how best to tell him, when Santa looked over his shoulder at the screen.

"Ho, ho, ho!" he boomed, sounding not at all unlike a policeman who has just caught a bloke with a bag marked 'swag' climbing out of a window. "I hadn't realised you'd been so naughty, Gordon. And after all the things you asked for at the store this afternoon! I can't believe it's really you."

"Nor can I," muttered Gordon. "I mean it isn't," he added. "It's a fix! I want a recount!"

Santa peered at him with a look he usually reserved for the elves' shop steward.

"I mean," said Gordon, pointing at the screen, "I'm only forty-five centimetres tall. I can't even reach a pillar box slot, let alone drop stink bombs into one!"

"He's got a point there," admitted Rudolph. "And look at his presents listing. Since when did we leave people mouldy tangerines and used, soggy teabags?"

"Hmmm. I could've punched it up wrongly, I suppose," said Santa. "Here, I'll try again." *Tac tacca tackitty tac!* Phillip's file scrolled onto the screen. "Well, nothing wrong with that one. Hmmm, Demi Moore. Don't think I can manage that one..."

"Wait, look!" gasped Gordon. Phillip's file was changing before their eyes. Out went all his good deeds and up came a lot of well, to be quite frank, despicable ones instead.

"It looks like you've got an illegal hacker in your system," said Gordon in hushed tones.

"And look," said Rudolph, "he's punching up another file. M...A...U..."

Across London, in a darkened den, the hunched figure of Maurice Mole sat silhouetted against a flickering VDU, chuckling to himself as usual as he tapped away on a computer keyboard.

Ha, ha, ha, hee, ho, ho! At least I've fixed that gopher and his beaming chum once and for all! Wait until they open their presents in the morning. Ho, ho, ho! What a surprise they'll get. Now I'll ensure myself a lifetime of Merry Christmases into the bargain...just access *my* file..."

Tap tap tappetty tap etc.

"Eh, what's this? One rotten selection box, and I'll bet it hasn't even got a game on the back! Well, we'll soon see about that!" *Tap tap tap!* "Let's see...one skateboard plus accessories, ten boxes of chocolate covered worms...heh, heh, heh!"

Back at the sleigh, Gordon watched Maurice's awful file turn into a glowing report.

Santa watched in horror. "We'll soon see about this!" he blustered. "Rudolph? Prepare for take-off!"

"But how are you going to find him?" asked Gordon.

"Left us his address so we could deliver his presents, didn't he?" said Santa as the sleigh rose into the air. Even though it was powered by magic, they didn't arrive until they'd got there, and they crept down into the den to surprise Maurice, who was still tapping away at his presents list on the computer.

"Aha!" said Rudolph.

"Ho, ho!" said Santa.

"Maurice!" said Gordon.

"Ak!" was all Maurice could say.

"Caught you floppy disked!" said Rudolph.

"Red-handed!" added Santa.

"Red-*pawed*!" corrected Gordon.

"Er...I don't suppose anyone would care for a cup of hot chocolate and a mince pie, would they?" said Maurice carelessy.

"I'm very disappointed in you, Maurice Mole," boomed Santa. "The results of your greedy meddling could have been catastrophic! I really don't know what I'm going to do with you!"

Rudolph whispered in Santa's ear.

"Ho, ho! A capital idea," exclaimed Santa. "You're going to set all the files straight, then you're coming with us, Maurice."

"I am?"

"You are, so don't dawdle. We've got a lot of work to do tonight. We'll drop you off at Phillip's house, Gordon. How's that?"

"Er...fine," said Gordon. "Just fine."

Gordon woke up in Phillip's spare bedroom.

"What a strange dream," he yawned as he got up and put on his dressing gown. Then he remembered it was Christmas morning. "Yippee!" he cried, rushing downstairs. Under the Christmas tree he found a pile of presents. He was about to start opening them when he spotted his instant camera. Lying beside it was a photograph. He picked it up. It was a bit out of focus, but surely that looked like a bit of antler, and there...a piece of mince pie and a hoof! And that bit in the corner — could it be white whiskers? Maybe it hadn't been a dream after all!

The label on a large present caught his eye: *to Gordon with many thanks and much gratitude — SC and R.* Scarcely able to contain his excitement, Gordon tore off the wrapping to reveal a brand new changeformer robot.

"Wow!" said Gordon.

Just then, Phillip came into the room. "Morning, Gordon," he yawned. "Merry Christmas!"

"Yes, isn't it?" said Gordon, tucking the photograph into his dressing gown pocket. "Isn't it just!"

And what of Maurice Mole, how was he spending his Christmas? He was spending it at the North Pole, sweeping up the workshops and washing out the elves' paintbrushes ready for next year.